Who ever heard of a tiger in a pink hat?!

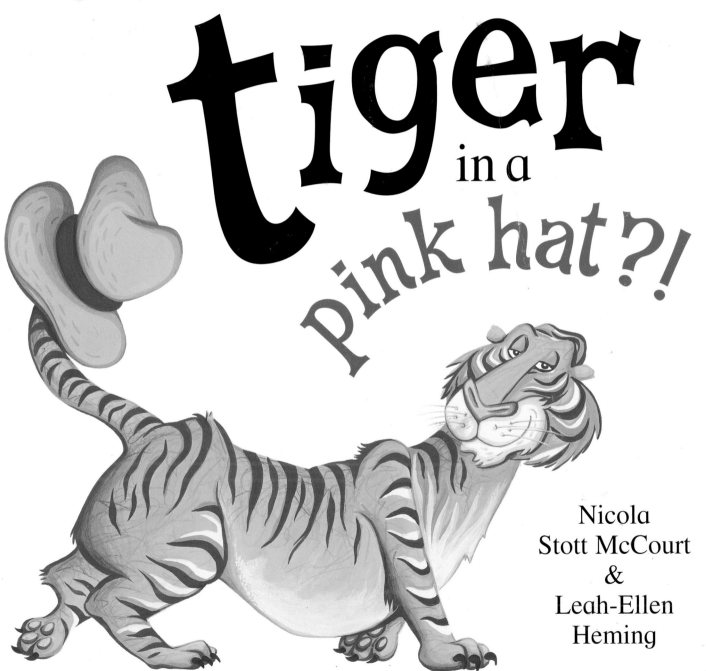

Nicola
Stott McCourt
&
Leah-Ellen
Heming

meadowside
CHILDREN'S BOOKS

One day a tiger went shopping.

The tiger bought
a pink hat.

Fancy that, **a pink hat!**

Who ever heard of a tiger
in a pink hat?

Next the tiger bought
a stripy umbrella.

Well I never,
a stripy umbrella!

Who ever heard of a tiger with
a stripy umbrella?

Next the tiger bought some green gloves.

Heavens above,
green
gloves!

Who ever heard of a tiger
wearing green gloves?

Next the tiger bought
a banana split.

I don't believe it,
**a banana
split!**

Who ever heard of a tiger eating
a banana split?

Next the tiger bought
some French perfume.

You're joking I presume,

French perfume?!

Who ever heard
of a tiger wearing
French perfume?

Next the tiger bought some roller skates.

Let me get this straight,
roller skates?!

Who ever heard of a tiger wearing roller skates?

Next the tiger bought
a diamond ring.

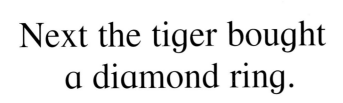

How amazing,
a diamond ring!

Who ever heard of a tiger wearing
a diamond ring?

Next the tiger bought
a red sports car.

How bizarre,
a red sports car!
Who ever heard of a tiger driving
a red sports car?

Next the tiger
bought a fur coat.

Wow, take note,
a fur coat!

Who ever heard
of a tiger in a
fur coat?!

Well, actually, I have!

For Mr McCourt
and my little men

N.M.

Pour mon ami Vincent

L.E.H.

First published in 2007
by Meadowside Children's Books
185 Fleet Street London EC4A 2HS
www.meadowsidebooks.com

A CIP catalogue record for this book
is available from the British Library
10 9 8 7 6 5 4 3 2
Printed in Indonesia